First published by Parragon in 2013
Parragon
Chartist House
15–17 Trim Street
Bath BA1 1HA, UK
www.parragon.com

Written by Margaret Wise Brown
Illustrated by Antoine Corbineau

Edited by Michael Diggle
Designed by Alex Dimond
Production by Jonathan Wakeham

ISBN 978-1-4723-1795-7

Printed in China

The DIGGERS

PaRragon

Bath · New York · Singapore · Hong Kong · Cologne · Delhi
Melbourne · Amsterdam · Johannesburg · Shenzhen

DIG
DIG
DIG

A mole was digging a hole.

DIG
DIG
DIG

A dog was digging a hole,
under a stone to bury a bone.

DIG DIG DIG

A worm was digging a hole.

He swallowed the ground,

as he wiggled around,

and ate his way toward home.

DIG

DIG

DIG

A rabbit was
digging a hole.

Next to a mouse,
who was digging a house,

in a little warm hole
in the ground.

DIG

DIG

DIG

A pirate was digging a hole.

A hole in the sand
to bury his gold,

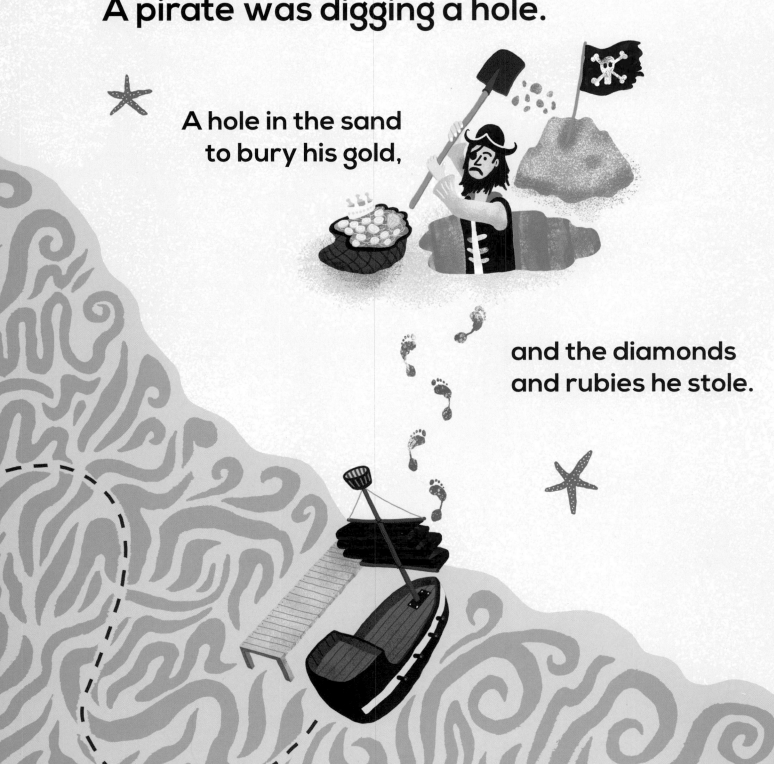

and the diamonds
and rubies he stole.

DIG DIG DIG

In the city, a man was digging a hole.

Monday he dug,

Tuesday he dug,

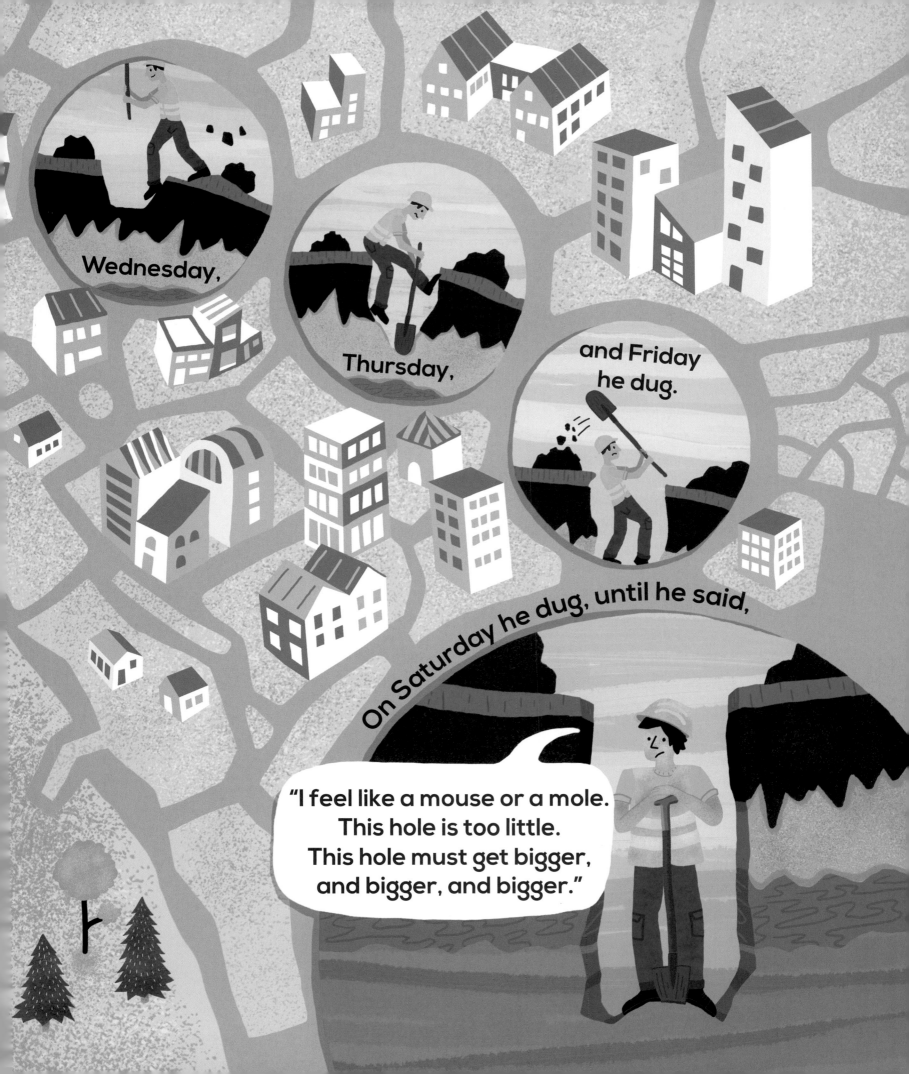

And then came the big digger,
    made by a man to dig deeper and bigger.

To scoop up stones,
and find dinosaur bones,
and cavemen's homes,
and buried gnomes.

DIG
DIG
DIG
The shovel dug its way.
Night after night,
day after day,

it dug.

And a great big hole ran under the city,
under a river,
and into the bright green country.

A man put a
train in the hole.

And the train ran under the street.
Under the city, under the river, until

it popped out of
the hole into bright
green country.

It went past ducks and geese,
and donkeys and cows,
and sheep and fields
of galloping horses.

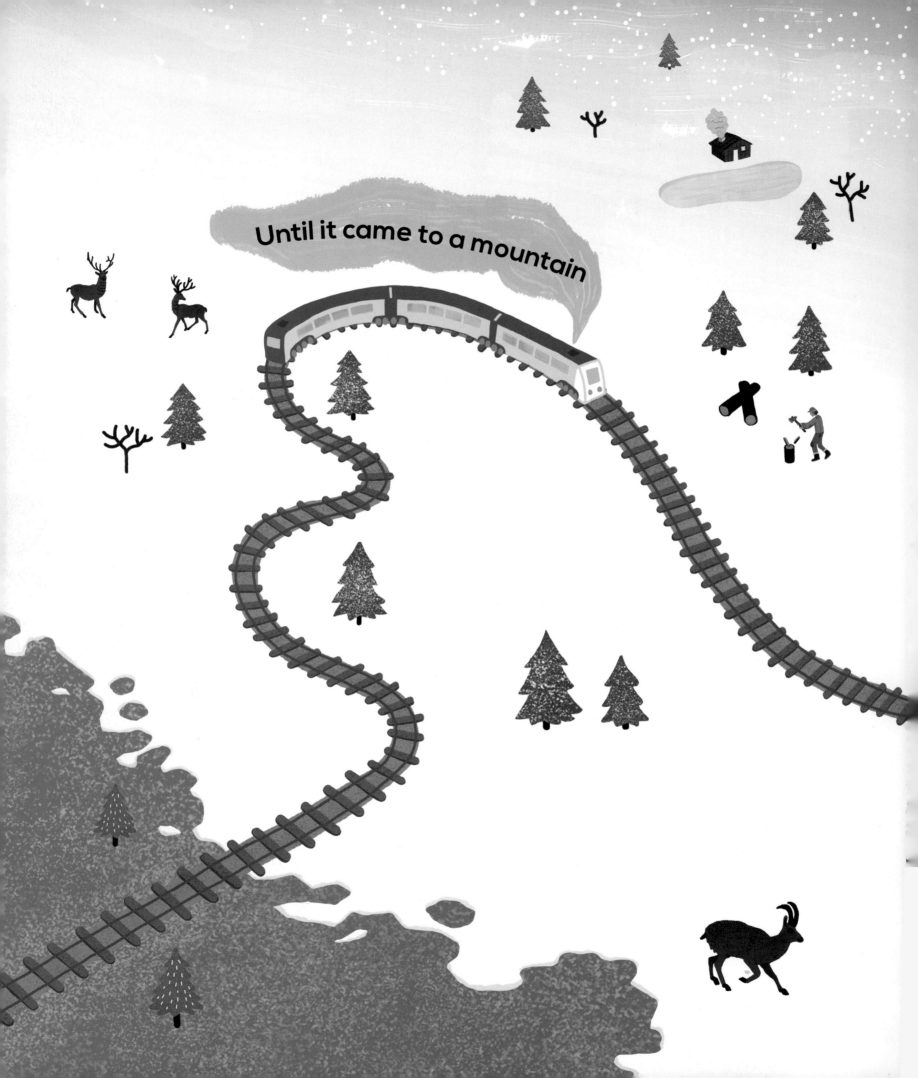

Until it came to a mountain

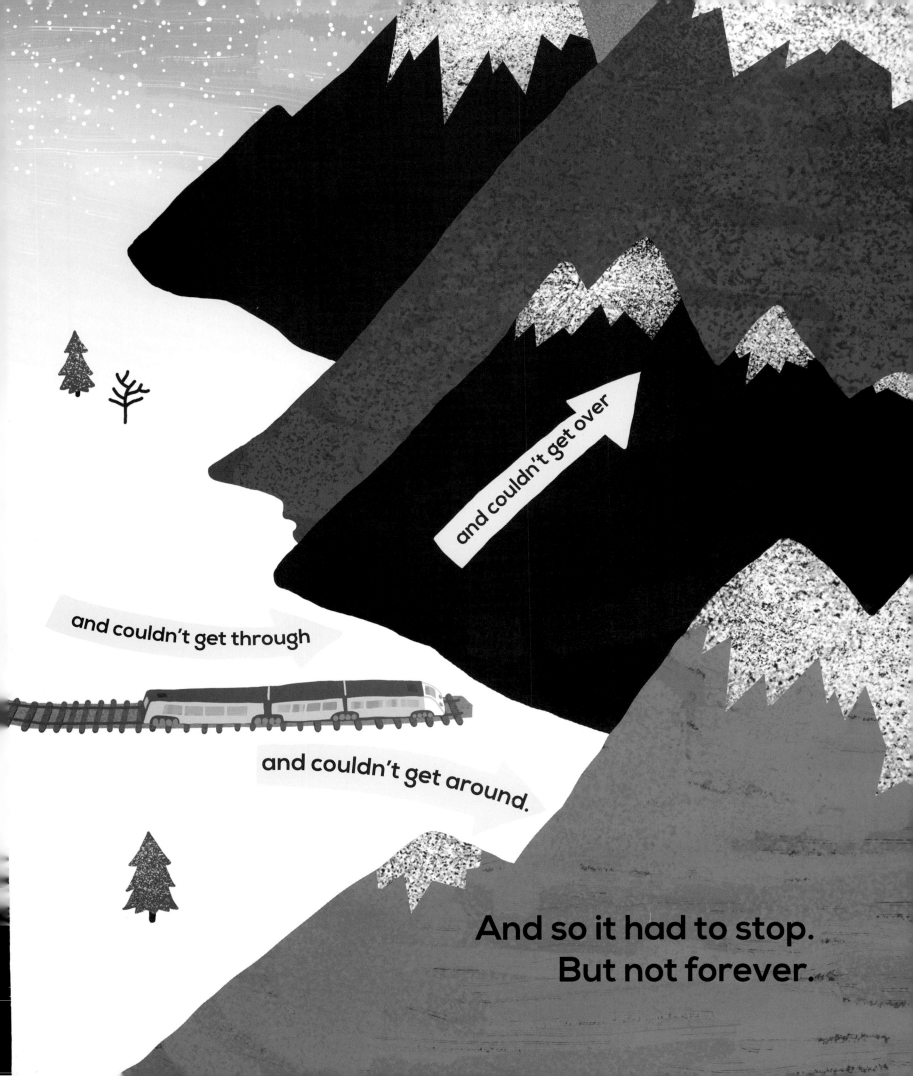

and couldn't get over

and couldn't get through

and couldn't get around.

And so it had to stop.
But not forever.

For down the track came another train.
And on the last car rode the great digger.

Under the mountain it dug away,
night after night, day after day.

Until, with one last bite
it came to daylight on the
other side of the mountain.

And soon the train came through the mountain and onto the great green plain beyond.

And on went the train,
on and on,
down its long steel track.

And the smoke trailed back,
and back,
and back.